Stick

The Very Hungry Caterpillar's
BUGS
Sticker & Colouring Book

Your adventure starts here!
Can you find a sticker of

The Very Hungry
Caterpillar

to stick on
this branch?

This book belongs to ....

PUFFIN

Mini Marvels

There are thousands of different types of bugs!
Can you use your stickers to fill this woodland scene
with some of the creepy-crawlies that live in our world?

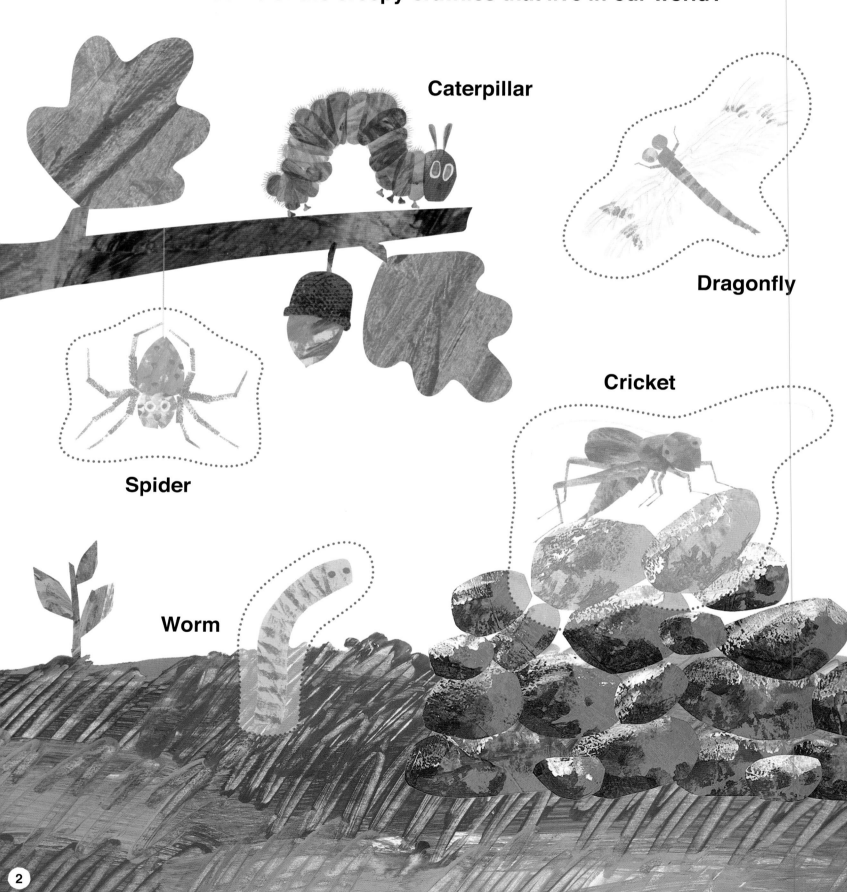

Caterpillar

Dragonfly

Cricket

Spider

Worm

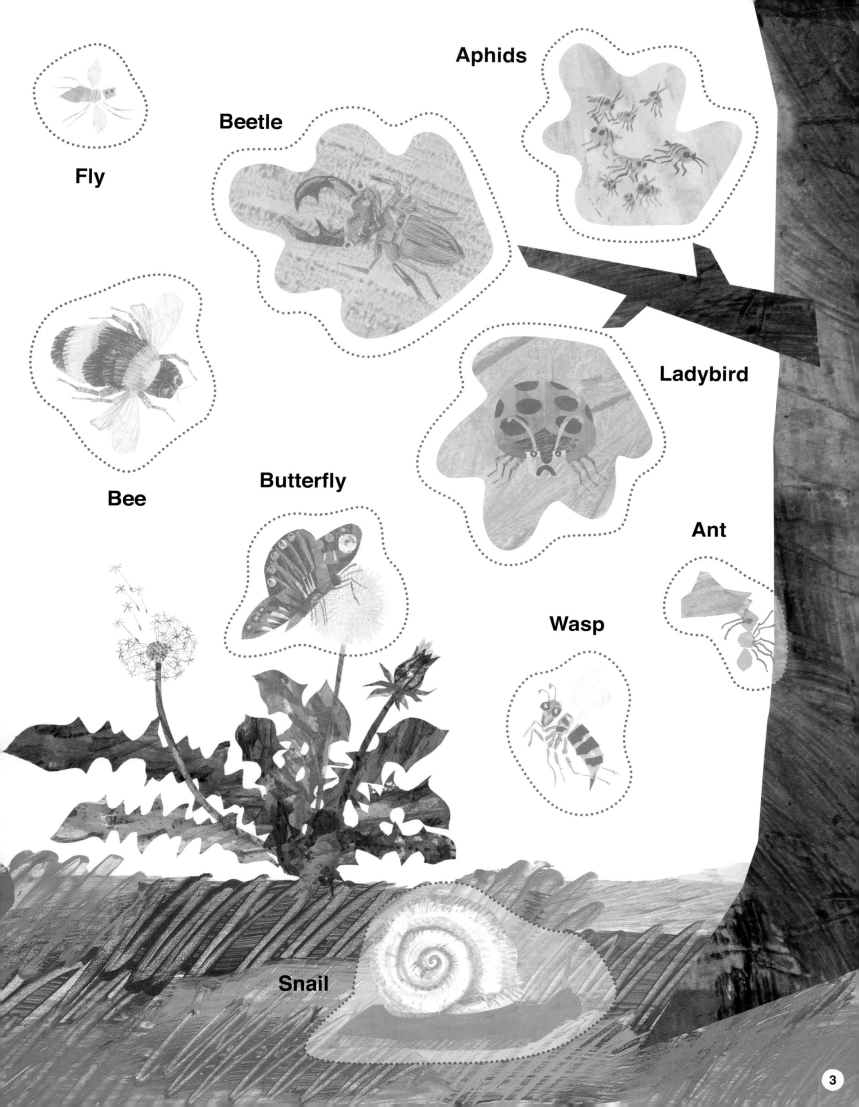

Fly

Beetle

Aphids

Bee

Butterfly

Ladybird

Ant

Wasp

Snail

Stick

Draw

Spinning Spiders

**Spiders spin sticky webs to catch bugs to eat.
Can you join the dots to finish this spider's web?
Then, can you use your sticker to put
the spider on the web?**

Can you add stickers of the flies the spider has caught?

Discover

Guess What?

Spiders are very busy – they usually spin a new web every day!

Up and Away

Many bugs have wings, and they use them to zip and zoom around us every day!
Use your stickers to fill the sky with fantastic flying bugs.

Stick

A Bee's Story

**Bees collect nectar from flowers to make honey.
Can you use your stickers to complete the story?**

start here

1

The bee leaves the **hive** to find flowers.

4

The bee flies back out to find more **flowers** and our story starts again.

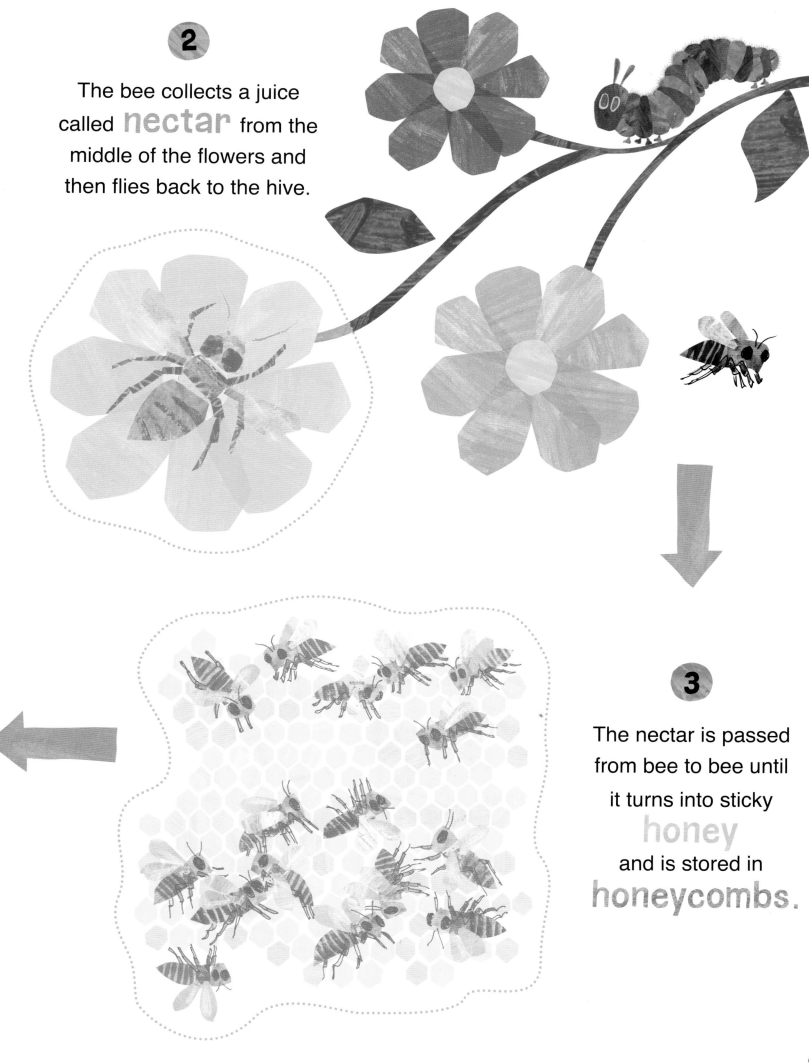

2

The bee collects a juice called **nectar** from the middle of the flowers and then flies back to the hive.

3

The nectar is passed from bee to bee until it turns into sticky **honey** and is stored in **honeycombs.**

Spots and Stripes

Bugs often have all sorts of bright colours and patterns.

Can you use

black

to colour in the spots on this ladybird?

Can you use

yellow

to colour in the stripes on this bee?

Help Out!

Bees get very thirsty. Help to look after them by putting out some water near flower beds for them to drink!

Can you use your
favourite colours and stickers
to decorate this beetle with
your own pattern?

SticK

Draw

Slithering Snail

Snails move very slo-o-o-o-wly and leave a silvery trail wherever they go. Can you follow the dotted line with a pencil to find out where this snail went? Put the snail sticker at the end of the trail.

start here

Discover

Guess What?

Snails don't have ears, so they can't hear anything!

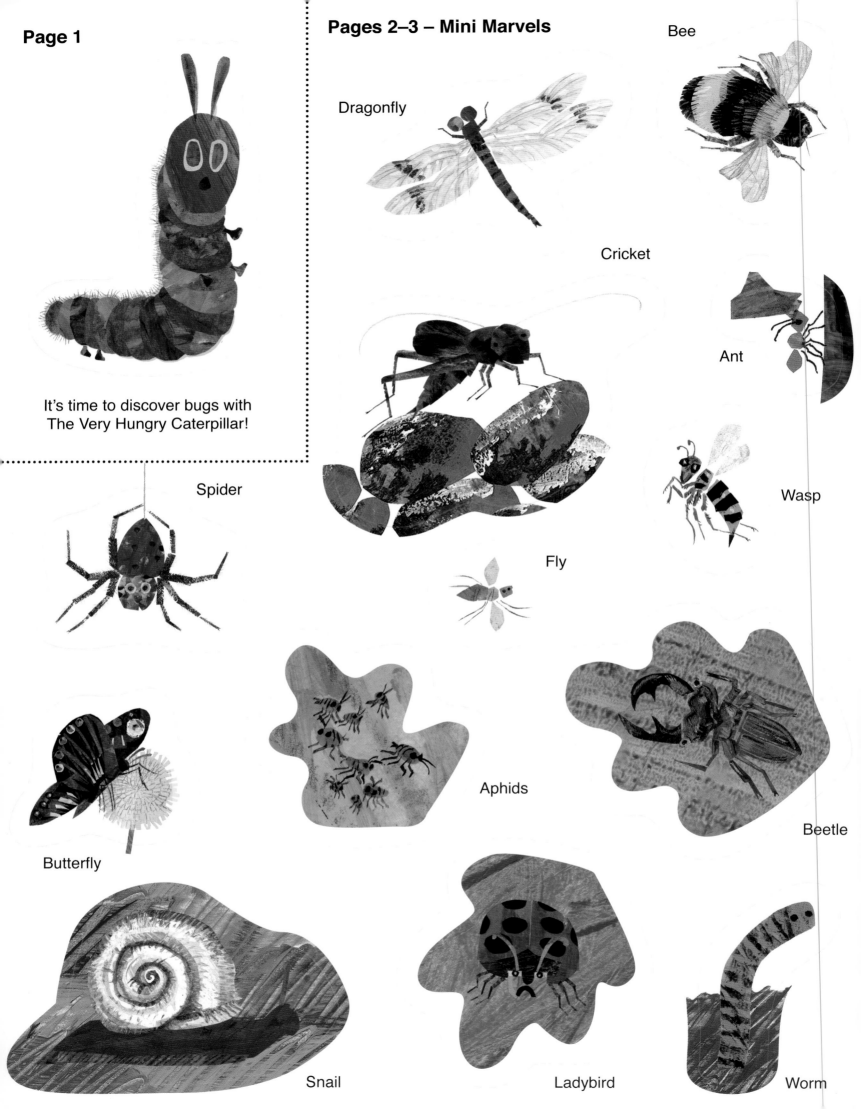

Pages 2–3 – Mini Marvels

Bee

Dragonfly

Cricket

Ant

It's time to discover bugs with The Very Hungry Caterpillar!

Spider

Wasp

Fly

Aphids

Beetle

Butterfly

Snail

Ladybird

Worm

Pages 4–5 – Spinning Spiders

Can you stick the spider on to the web?

Can you stick the flies on to the web?

Pages 6–7 – Up and Away

Locust

Butterfly

Bee

Butterfly

Ladybird

Butterfly

Dragonfly

Dragonfly

Fly

Wasp

™ & © 2019 Eric Carle LLC

Pages 8–9 – A Bee's Story

1

2

3

4

Pages 10–11 – Spots and Stripes

Triangles

Squares

Pages 10–11 – Spots and Stripes
(continued)

Spots

Rectangles

Stripes

Pages 12–13 – Slithering Snail

Bird

Dog

Cat

Snail

Pages 14–15 – A Caterpillar's Tale

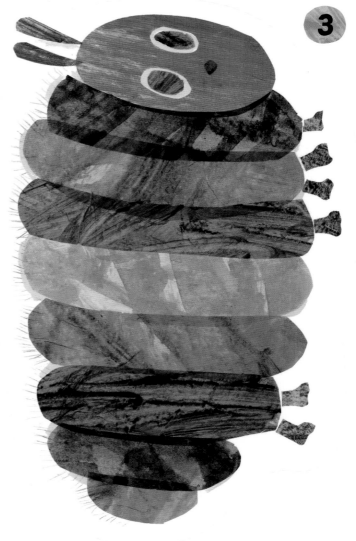

3

Pages 16–17
Brillliant Butterfly

Flowers

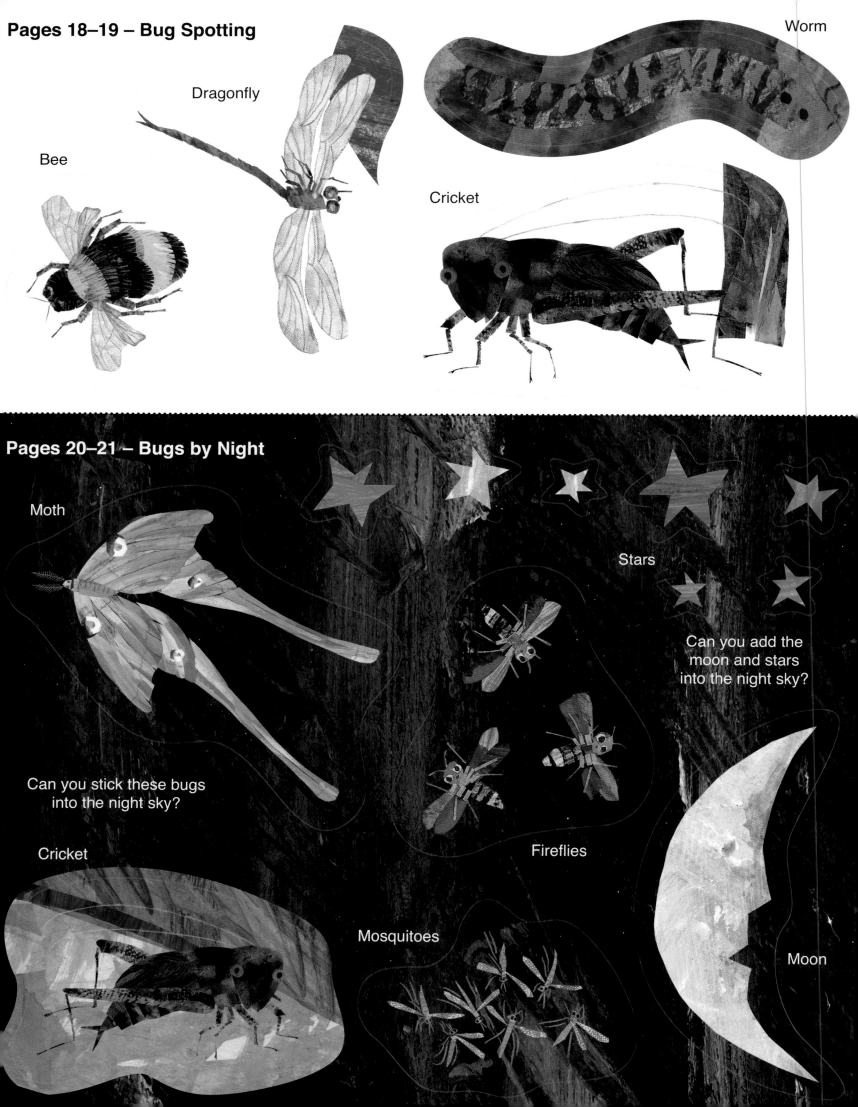

Pages 18–19 – Bug Spotting

Dragonfly

Worm

Bee

Cricket

Pages 20–21 – Bugs by Night

Moth

Stars

Can you add the
moon and stars
into the night sky?

Can you stick these bugs
into the night sky?

Cricket

Fireflies

Mosquitoes

Moon

Pages 22–23 – Bug Facts

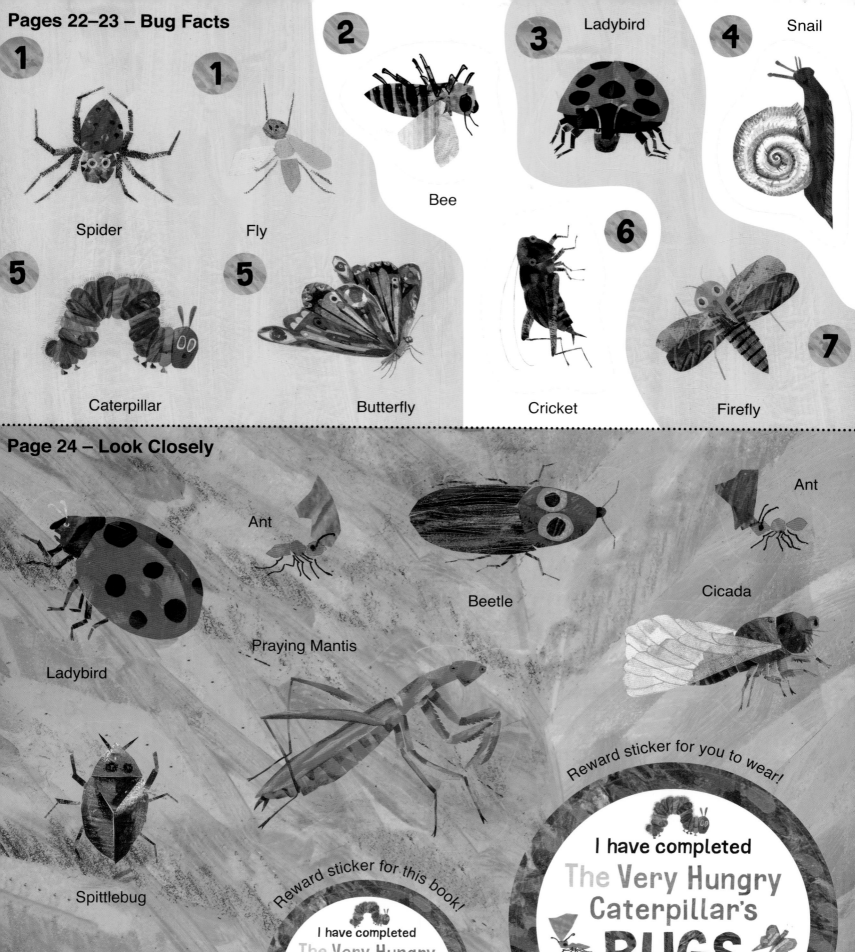

1 Spider

1 Fly

2 Bee

3 Ladybird

4 Snail

5 Caterpillar

5 Butterfly

6 Cricket

7 Firefly

Page 24 – Look Closely

Ant

Ant

Beetle

Cicada

Praying Mantis

Ladybird

Spittlebug

Caterpillar

Reward sticker for this book!

I have completed
The Very Hungry
Caterpillar's
BUGS
Adventure

Reward sticker for you to wear!

I have completed
The Very Hungry
Caterpillar's
BUGS
Adventure

Next, can you use your stickers to see who else is in the garden?

Stick

Colour

A Caterpillar's Tale

**Can you find a sticker of a big caterpillar?
Then, can you use your colours to complete
The Very Hungry Caterpillar's story?**

1

The Very Hungry
Caterpillar hatches
from a little egg.

2

He's already very hungry!
What will he eat first?

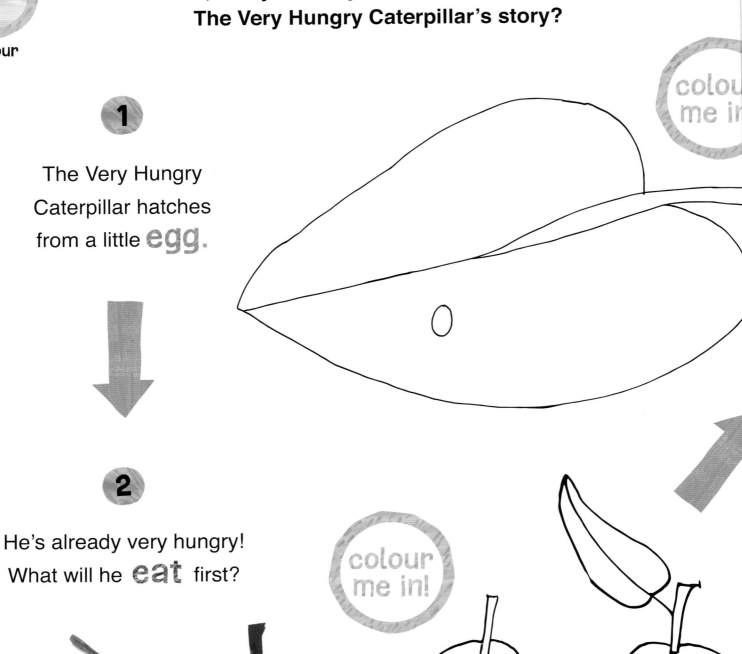

colour
me in!

colour
me in!

3

Now The Very Hungry Caterpillar is much, much **bigger...**

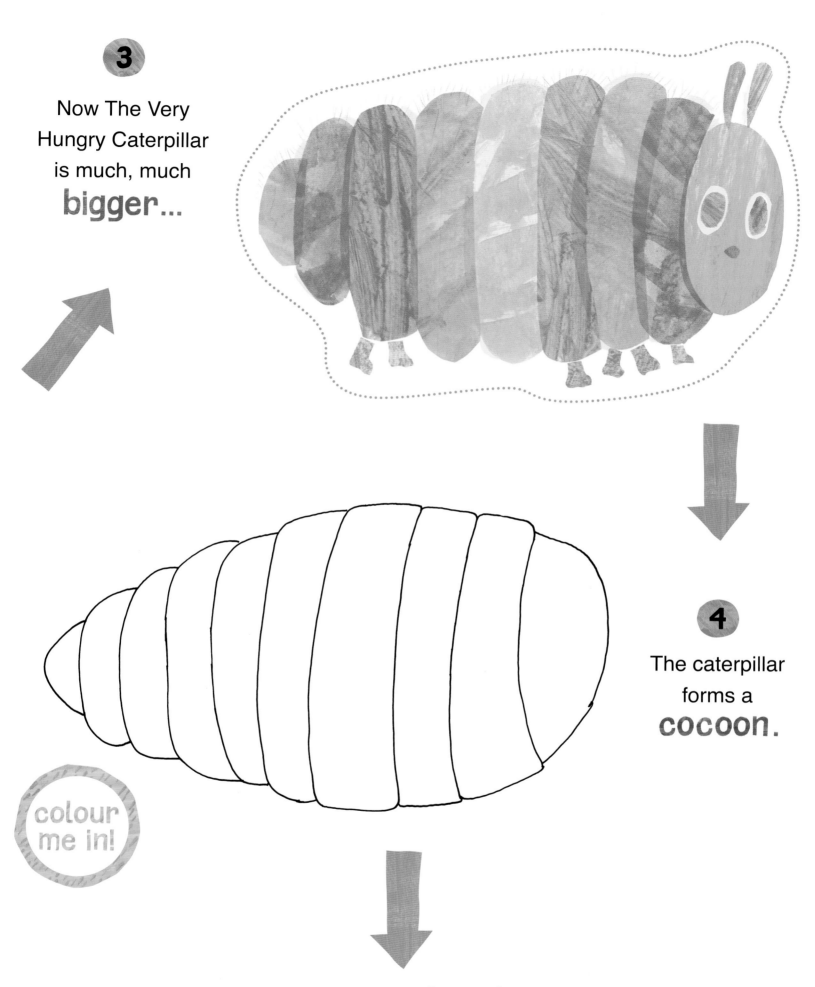

4

The caterpillar forms a **cocoon.**

colour me in!

Turn the page to see **what happens next...**

Stick

Colour

Beautiful Butterfly

**The caterpillar has become a brilliant butterfly!
Can you use your favourite colours to finish
decorating this butterfly?**

Then, use your stickers to add flowers.

colour me in!

Discover

Help Out!

You can help to feed butterflies by planting flowers in your garden or window box!

Bug Spotting

Bugs can live in many different places. Can you use your stickers to put these bugs and creepy-crawlies where they love to be?

Flowers

Bees are attracted to colourful petals.

Soil

Worms love cool soil underground.

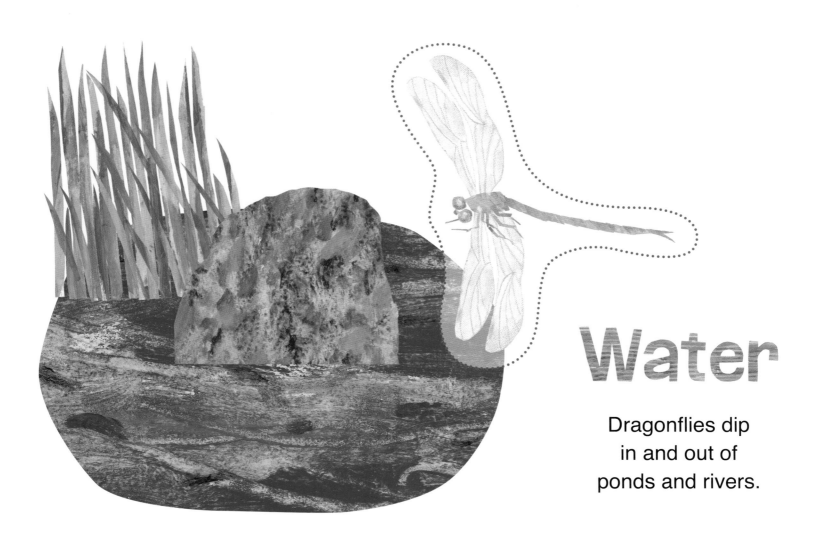

Water

Dragonflies dip
in and out of
ponds and rivers.

Grass

Crickets like to hide
in the long grass.

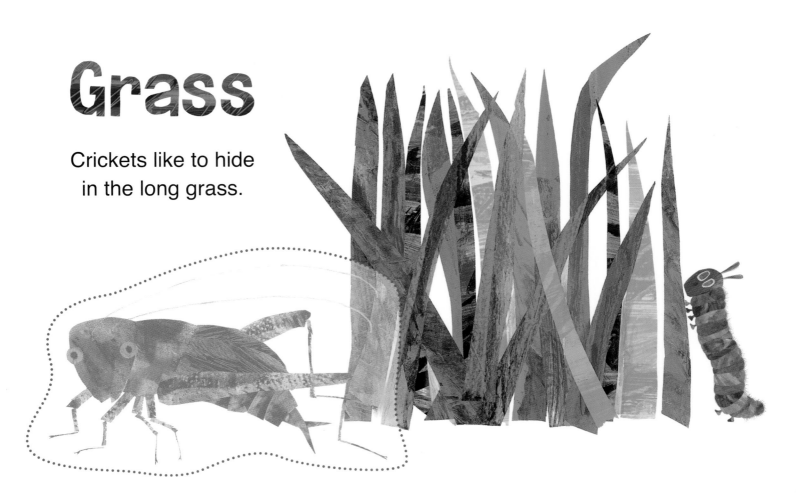

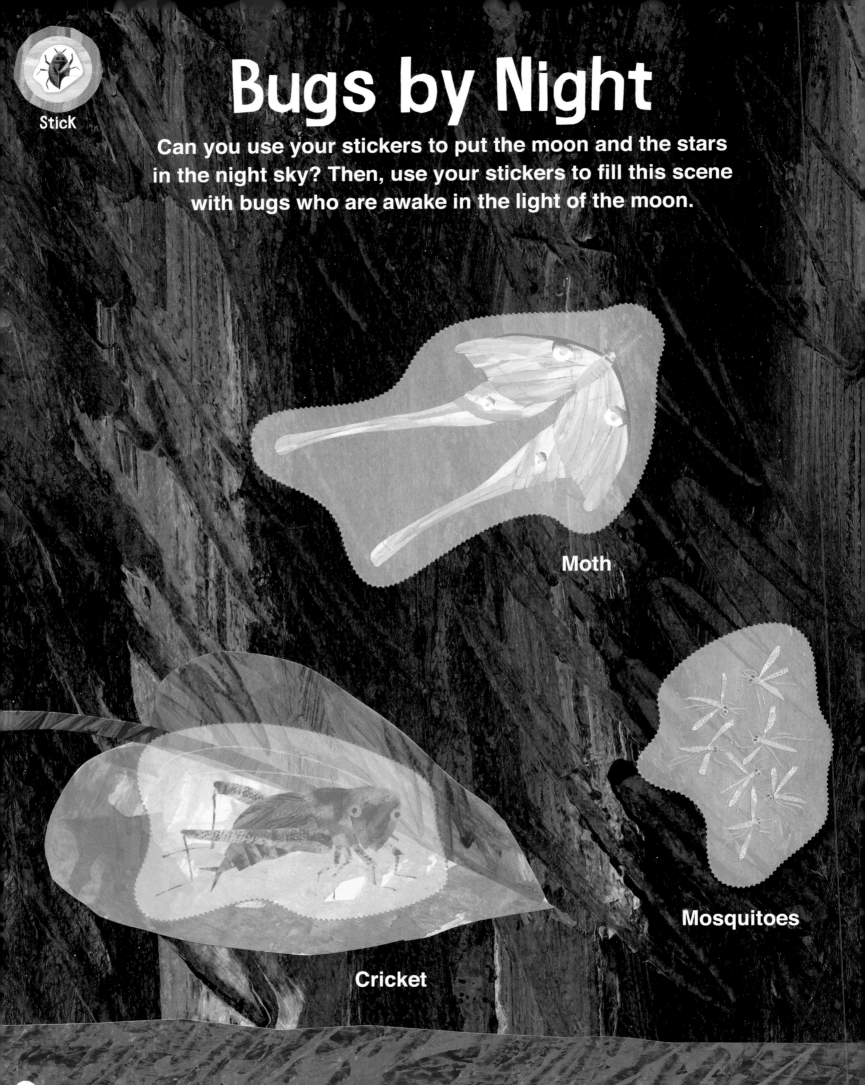

Bugs by Night

Can you use your stickers to put the moon and the stars in the night sky? Then, use your stickers to fill this scene with bugs who are awake in the light of the moon.

Stick

Moth

Cricket

Mosquitoes

Guess What?

Moths are coloured to blend in with their environment — this is called camouflage.

Fireflies

Bug Facts

Now you've found out all about bugs, can you use your stickers to fill in the missing words in these sentences?

Stick

1 A  catches a in its web.

2 A  makes honey in a beehive.

3 A  is covered in spots.

4  A moves very slo-o-o-o-wly.

5  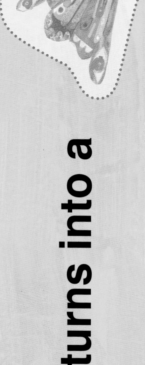 A turns into a .

6  A likes to hide in the long grass.

7  A comes out at night.

Look Closely

If you look closely, bugs are everywhere! Can you use your stickers to choose some bugs to live on this leaf?

I have completed
The Very Hungry
Caterpillar's
BUGS
Adventure

Well done!
Can you find your very
special stickers? You can
stick one here and wear
the other one with pride!